Costumes designed by Donna Beston
Photography by Tim Ridley
Illustrations by Strawberrie Donnelly
The publisher would like to thank the Flower Fairy models: Lily Dang,
Dusty Fairweather, Helen Hickman, Charlotte King, Saskia McCracken,
India Pulbrook, Elishaba Ramadeen and Rachel Winton.

FREDERICK WARNE
Published by the Penguin Group
Penguin Books Ltd, 27 Wrights Lane, London W8 5TZ, England
Penguin Putnam Inc., 375 Hudson Street, New York, NY 10014, USA
Penguin Books Australia Ltd, Ringwood, Victoria, Australia
Penguin Books Canada Ltd, 10 Alcorn Avenue, Toronto, Ontario, Canada M4V 3B2
Penguin Books (N.Z.) Ltd, 182-190 Wairau Road, Auckland 10, New Zealand

Penguin Books Ltd, Registered Offices: Harmondsworth, Middlesex, England

First published 1999 by Frederick Warne

1 3 5 7 9 10 8 6 4 2

Original illustrations copyright © The Estate of Cicely Mary Barker, 1923, 1925,
1926, 1934, 1940, 1944
New reproductions copyright © The Estate of Cicely Mary Barker, 1990

ISBN 0 7232 4495 2

Colour reproduction by Saxon Photolitho Ltd, Norwich
Printed in Singapore by Imago Publishing Ltd

FLOWER FAIRIES ™

FANCY DRESS BOOK

Based on the illustrations by

CICELY MARY BARKER

FREDERICK WARNE

CONTENTS

CONTENTS

INTRODUCTION

What little girl does not relish dressing up as a fairy? Perfect for playtime or party time, these irresistible costumes are a dream come true for Flower Fairies fans of all ages. In these ethereal frocks, dazzling wings and sparkling tiaras, children will be ready to flutter away to fairyland. There are hours of imaginative fun to be had skipping around a fairy circle, dancing at the fairy ball or casting spells with a glittering wand. Best of all, you do not need a handful of fairy dust to magic up these costumes!

Hand-made costumes are so much more original than store-bought costumes, and children will enjoy helping you choose colours and fabrics. Not only is sewing satisfying, it is also economical and ensures a customised fit, as each costume can be adapted for a child of any age or size. Whether you are a beginner or an expert dressmaker, there is a range of beautiful costumes, from simple to challenging, to suit your ability level. Designed with busy parents in mind, these costumes do not take long to make and require only easy-to-find materials. Including templates, step-by-step illustrations and clear instructions, this beautiful book makes creating costumes foolproof.

The costumes featured in this book are inspired by Cicely Mary Barker's classic Flower Fairy illustrations. Born in Croydon, South London in 1895, Cicely Mary Barker showed artistic talent from an early age. Encouraged by her parents, she had a set of postcards accepted for publication by the time she was 15 years old. The first Flower Fairies book was published in 1923, bringing Cicely commercial success and international acclaim as an artist. She went on to publish a total of seven Flower Fairies books, which feature her poems and delightful watercolour paintings of children and flowers.

For her twenty-first birthday, Cicely was given a copy of Dion Clayton Calthrop's *English Costume* by her grandmother. Using the book as reference, Cicely designed costumes for her Flower Fairy models, who were pupils at her elder sister's kindergarten. In her garden studio Cicely kept a large chest filled with materials. For each Flower Fairy, Cicely made a new costume that reflected the colour, texture and shape of the flower. She also constructed wings from twigs and gauze for her models to wear. Once the picture was finished, Cicely would meticulously unpick the stitches of the costume in order to reuse the material. In this book, we have replicated Cicely's costume designs as closely as possible, paying attention to the details that make her pictures so special.

BASIC TECHNIQUES

MEASUREMENTS

This diagram shows you how to take a child's measurements. When transferring the measurements to fabric, allow approximately 4 cm (2 in) extra for seams, hems and ease of movement.

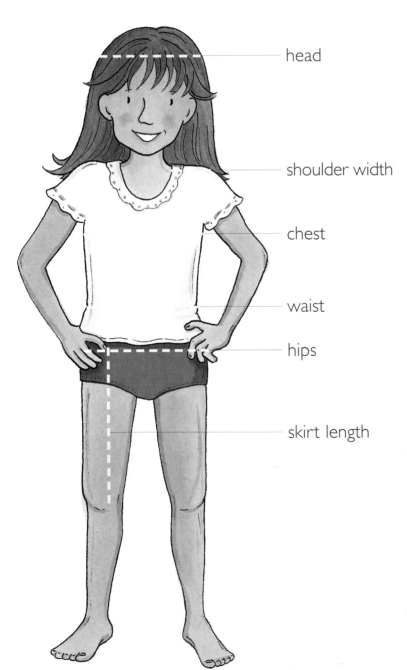

head

shoulder width

chest

waist

hips

skirt length

COPYING FROM A GARMENT

When making tops and underslips, you can take a short cut and copy dimensions from an item of the child's clothing. Place the garment wrong-side out on the back of folded fabric, draw around it with tailor's chalk, and cut out the pieces.

MAKING A WAISTBAND

Cut a piece of waistband elastic to fit the child's waist measurement minus 10 cm (4 in), then check it for fit. Cut a strip of fabric to fit the child's waist and approximately 10 cm (4 in) wide. Press a fold line lengthwise along the centre of the strip. Stitch along the long, non-folded edge, catching both layers, to make a channel. Attach a safety pin to one end of the elastic and thread it through the channel, ruching up the fabric as you work. Pin the ends of the elastic to the ends of the channel, then sew the ends of the elastic together to form a band. Sew the ends of the channel to finish the waistband.

Velcro® fastenings

Separate the two halves of a Velcro® tab. Position one half of the Velcro® about 3 mm (¹/₈ in) from the fabric's edge and secure with a few stitches. Position the other half of the Velcro® on the opposite half of the closure, on the reverse side of the fabric, so the two halves match up. Sew the Velcro® in place.

Fabrics

When choosing fabric for a costume, there are many factors to consider, from the fabric's weight and fibre, to the style and design. Certain fabrics must be handled carefully to avoid costly mishaps.

When cutting out **stretch fabrics**, such as velour and jersey, always make sure that the stretch runs across the width of the fabric.

Fine, **sheer fabrics**, such as organza, chiffon and net, should be cut carefully with sharp scissors on a non-slippery surface, such as a blanket or sheet.

When cutting out **PVC**, use masking tape to hold the pattern pieces in place. You can also use tape instead of pins to hold PVC pieces together when sewing.

Satin, silk and taffeta fray easily, so leave a large seam allowance. After cutting the fabric, oversew the edges by machine immediately.

Seams and stitches

For a hard-wearing, professional-looking garment, choose a needle and seam to suit the fabric and purpose.

Choose a seam with minimum layers if sewing a bulky fabric and use an enclosed seam when sewing flimsy material.

Zigzag stitching on a sewing machine is a good way to neaten up raw edges and prevent fraying.

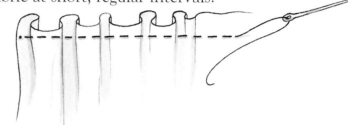

A simple hand stitch, **running stitch** involves passing the needle through the fabric at short, regular intervals.

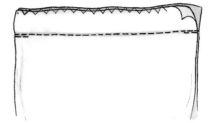

Hemming stitch produces a neat, folded edge. For the best effect, the tiny stitches must be sewn at short, even intervals.

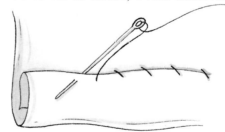

Slipstitch is useful for joining two folded edges almost invisibly. This hand stitch is useful for sewing an opening closed.

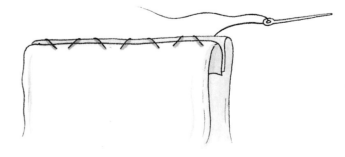

WINGS

The wings for each fairy costume have a different shape, but they can all be made using the same method. This technique involves making two sets of wings—a large top set and a smaller lower set—which are combined to make sturdy wings that will not flop. A wide variety of materials can be used to decorate the wings. Experiment with fabric paints, marker pens, acrylic paints, tissue paper, glitter glue and even nail varnish and doilies to achieve the desired effect. Because the comfortable, elastic straps can be worn inside the costume, the wings look realistic and children will forget they are wearing them.

MATERIALS:

❀ newspaper
❀ pencil or marker pen
❀ acetate (available from art shops)
❀ 2 cm (1 in) wide waistband elastic
❀ tape
❀ variety of decorative materials
❀ stapler
❀ glue gun

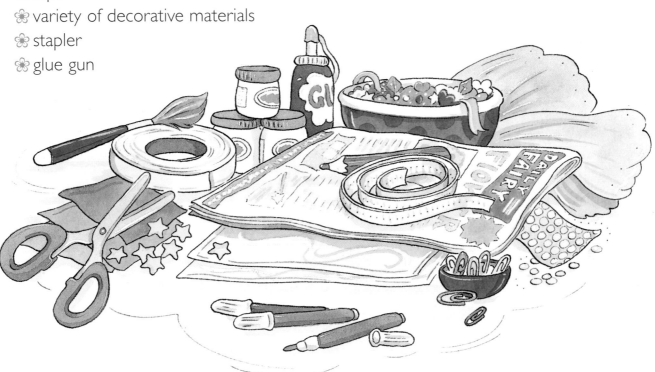

METHOD

1. Pleat a large sheet of newspaper concertina-style, then try drawing wings on the paper. You will need to make two wing patterns, one for the large and one for the small wings. When you are happy with the wings' size and shape, cut them out to make your patterns.

2. Unfold the large wing pattern and draw around it on to two large sheets of acetate, one on top of the other. Do the same for the small wing pattern. You will need to make four wings in total. Be sure to chose a quality of acetate that takes paint and marker pens.

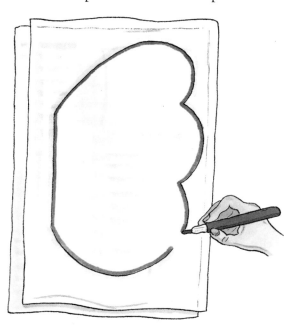

3. Using the picture of the fairy as your reference, paint and decorate the acetate wings accordingly. If you use strips of tissue paper or fine fabric, stick them on with a very diluted water and glitter glue solution. Remember to paint the wings in matching pairs.

4. When the paint is dry, cut out the wings and pleat each one into a fan shape. Each pleat should be about 2 cm (1 in) wide. If you wish to adjust the pleats, hold the fan in place with a paper clip. Staple the end of each fan to hold it in place.

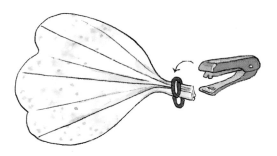

5. Tape the top pair of wings securely together at the stapled ends, then tape the bottom pair of wings together.

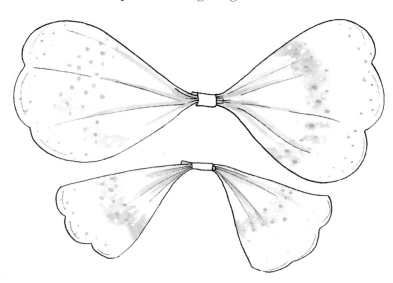

6. Join the top wings to the bottom wings using a hot glue gun or tape. Glue the two sets of wings together at a few points along the seam so they are firmly attached.

7. To make the straps, cut two lengths of soft, 2 cm (1 in) wide elastic. Each piece must be long enough to wrap around the child's shoulder and meet in the middle of the back.

8. Cut a strip of the fabric used for the costume, measuring about 10 x 25 cm (4 x 10 in). Fold the strip in half lengthwise and sew the long edges together, right sides facing. Turn the fabric tube right-side out. Sew a length of elastic to each end, pinch pleating the fabric to the width of the elastic, to make straps like a satchel's handle.

9. Tie the straps around the centre of the wings in a firm knot, ensuring that the front of the fabric is showing on the painted side of the wings.

10. Try the wings on the child. You may need to tighten the straps by tying another knot. If necessary, trim the wings to finish off the outline or to make them more manageable for the child to wear.

Fuchsia Fairy

Christmas Tree Fairy

Daisy Fairy

Buttercup Fairy

Marigold Fairy

Holly Fairy

Strawberry Fairy

Poppy Fairy

The Daisy Fairy

Come to me and play with me,
I'm the babies' flower;
Make a necklace gay with me,
Spend the whole long day with me,
Till the sunset hour.

I must say Good-night, you know,
Till tomorrow's playtime;
Close my petals tight, you know,
Shut the red and white, you know,
Sleeping till the daytime.

METHOD
Level – Easy ❀

The delicate daisy is known as the "babies' flower," and this adorable Daisy Fairy costume is ideally suited for young children. A green T-shirt, an elasticated, petal skirt, some creative painting and a daisy chain are all it takes to transform a mischievous toddler into the charming Daisy Fairy. This simple costume, designed for the wearer's comfort, perfectly captures the essence of the daisy flower with a minimum of sewing.

SIZE: Measurements and templates to fit a 2–3 year-old child.

MATERIALS:

❀ green T-shirt

❀ pink or red acrylic paint or marker pen

❀ silver glitter paint

❀ iridescent acrylic glitter glaze

❀ white pearlized dimensional paint

❀ white plastic-coated fabric (i.e. shower curtain fabric)

❀ soft waistband elastic, 1.5 cm (³/4 in) thick or a pair of white knickers

❀ cotton reel or sticky tape reel

❀ yellow embroidery thread

❀ green glossy, dimensional fabric paint

❀ white and green raffia

❀ 6 tacks

T-SHIRT

1. Mark a zigzag border around both sleeves and the waist of a green T-shirt and cut out along the edges.

2. Outline the zigzags on the sleeves and waist with glossy, green dimensional fabric paint. Leave the paint to dry.

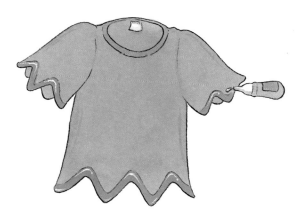

SKIRT

1. Measure the child's waist, then cut a piece of elastic two inches smaller than this measurement. Sew the ends of the elastic together to make a waistband.

2. Cut out a card template of the petal shape provided and mark 20 petals on to white shower curtain fabric in pencil.

3. Colour the tips of each petal with pink or red acrylic paint or marker pen.

4. Using your fingertip, spread iridescent glitter glaze thinly over each petal.

Outline around each petal with silver glitter paint, blending it with your fingertip.

5. Draw veins on each petal with white, pearlized dimensional paint. Leave the paint to dry for two to three hours, then cut out the petals.

6. Sew the petals on to the elastic waistband, making a small pinch pleat at the top of each petal and stretching the elastic out as you work.

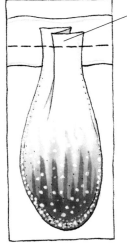

pinch pleat

DAISY CROWN

1. Press six tacks around the edge of a cotton reel or a small sticky tape reel at even intervals.

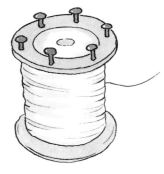

2. Wind white raffia around each of the tacks in a pinwheel design, as shown. Leaving the ends about 5 cm (2 in) long, loop them under the middle of the pinwheel and tie tightly on top.

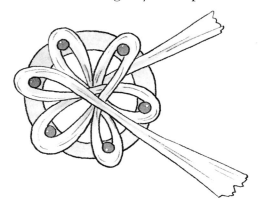

3. Using a darning needle, sew over the centre of the daisy, looping around all six petals with yellow embroidery thread. Loop the ends under the middle of the daisy and tie them off firmly.

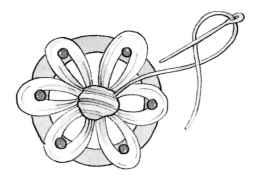

4. Cut the ends of the pinwheel's spokes away from the tacks. Spread open and flatten the raffia to make petals. Trim the edges of the petals, then colour the tips with a red marker pen. Repeat steps 1–4 until you have enough daisies to make a crown.

5. Cut a piece of green raffia long enough to fit around the child's head. Thread the raffia on to a darning needle and pass it through the back of the yellow stitches on a daisy.

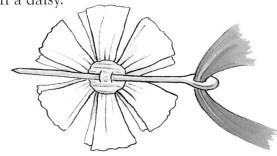

6. As you thread on the daisies, push them along the raffia so they are evenly spaced. Knot the green raffia after each daisy to keep the flowers in place.

7. When all of the daisies are strung on to the raffia, tie the ends of the raffia together to form the crown. You can also make a daisy necklace using the same technique.

WINGS

These translucent wings were made extra sturdy by covering the acetate with white plastic-coated fabric. After gluing the fabric wrong-side down to the sheet of acetate, proceed to draw around your template and make the wings using the method described on pages 12–15. These wings were decorated with streaks and swirls of black, yellow, turquoise and pink acrylic paint and given texture with veins of white pearlized, dimensional paint. The addition of iridescent acrylic glitter glaze makes the wings shimmer.

THE
MARIGOLD FAIRY

Great Sun above me in the sky,
So golden, glorious, and high,
My petals, see, are golden too;
They shine, but cannot shine like you.

I scatter many seeds around;
And where they fall upon the ground,
More Marigolds will spring, more flowers
To open wide in sunny hours.

It is because I love you so,
I turn to watch you as you go;
Without your light, no joy could be.
Look down, great Sun, and shine on me!

METHOD
Level – Easy ❀

With her green tunic setting off her bright orange petals, the Marigold Fairy looks as radiant as a beam of sunshine. Golden marigolds are popular in summer gardens, but this costume will be a favourite with fairy fans at any time of year. Wonderfully fun to make, this costume uses a fingerpainting technique to create abstract swirls and streaks. A marigold tucked jauntily behind the ear and a warm smile are the only accessories needed to complete this winning outfit!

SIZE: Measurements and templates to fit a 4–5 year-old child.

MATERIALS:

❀ 1 m (1 yd) green stretch jersey fabric or stretch velour

❀ Velcro®

❀ flower-making wire

❀ 50 cm (20 in) orange plastic-coated fabric (i.e. shower curtain or table cloth fabric)

❀ yellow, orange, dark green and gold glitter acrylic or fabric paints

❀ fabric glue

Petal Collar

1. Using the template provided, draw 14 petal shapes on to the right side of the orange plastic-coated fabric. Fingerpaint the petals with yellow, orange and gold glitter acrylic paints and allow to dry before cutting out the petals.

2. Spread fabric glue on the back of each petal. Stick the petals on to the wrong side of more orange plastic-coated fabric, sandwiching a piece of wire, bent into a U-shape, between each petal and the fabric.

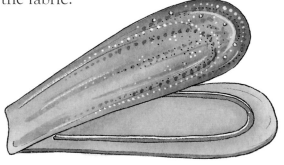

3. Allow the glue to dry, then cut out the petals. Both the front and back of each petal should show the right side of the fabric.

4. Measure around the child's neck. Cut out a strip of green fabric 10 cm (4 in) deep, adding 10 cm (4 in) to the neck measurement to accommodate the wrapover.

5. Fold the green strip in half lengthwise with right sides together. Sew along the length to close the seam.

6. Turn the collar right-side out and press. Tuck in the raw edges on each end about 1 cm ($^1/_2$ in) and press.

7. Sew a small Velcro® tab on to each end of the collar. The Velcro® pieces must be on opposite sides of the collar, so that the two ends overlap.

8. Lay seven petals, painted sides facing down, along the lower edge of the collar and sew in place.

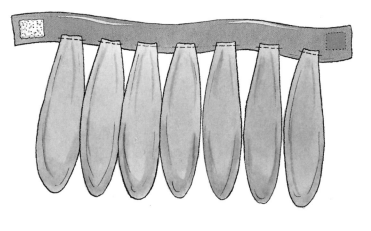

9. Position seven petals along the top edge of the collar, interspersed between the lower petals.

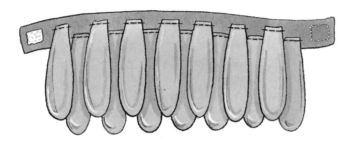

10. Sew the petals in place with their right sides facing down. When the collar is worn, the side on which the petals are attached should sit against the neck.

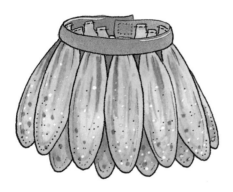

𝒯UNIC

1. Measure the child's length from shoulder to knee. Take the child's hip measurement and divide it in half. Mark two rectangles to these measurements on green fabric, adding an extra 10 cm (4 in) each way for ease of movement, then cut out the front and back of the tunic.

2. Lay the two fabric rectangles on newspaper and pin in place. Using dark green and gold paints, fingerpaint streaks on the right side of the fabric to produce a variegated colour effect. Unpin the fabric when the paint is dry.

3. Using the template provided, cut out two sleeve frill sections from green fabric and fingerpaint the frills in the same style as the tunic rectangles.

4. Fold the front rectangle in half and cut a shallow, rounded dip to allow for the front of the neck. Then fold the back rectangle in half and make a 25 cm (10 in) slit at the top of the fold, to make an opening on the back of the tunic.

5. Lay the two pieces on top of each other, right sides facing. Close the seam from the edge of each shoulder to the neckline.

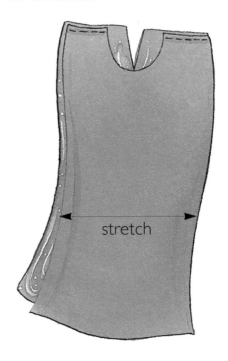

stretch

6. Sew loose running stitch along the straight edge of each sleeve frill. Pull the end of the thread to gather each sleeve frill.

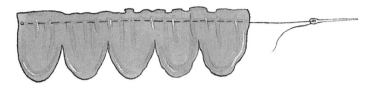

7. Pin a frill to each shoulder, matching the frill's centre to the shoulder seam. To make armholes, sew the frills from the shoulder seams along the sides of the tunic, about 15 cm (6 in) down on each side. The painted side of the frills should face the painted side of the tunic.

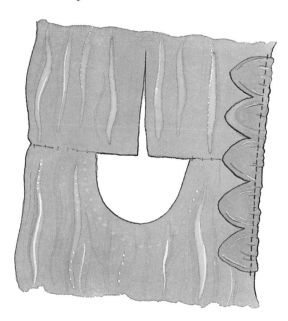

8. Close the side seams, sewing from below the armholes to the hem.

9. Turn the tunic right-side out and attach two small tabs of Velcro® to the opening at the back of the neck to fasten.

$\mathcal{W}$INGS

The Marigold Fairy's small, jagged wings, made following the method on pages 12–15, were fingerpainted with bold streaks and stripes of yellow, orange and black acrylic paint. Use the same paints that you used to decorate the collar petals and leave a bit of clear acetate showing through the stripes of colour. When the costume is worn, adjust the collar petals so they fall over the wings.

THE BUTTERCUP FAIRY

'Tis I whom children love the best;
My wealth is all for them;
For them is set each glossy cup
Upon each sturdy stem.

O little playmates whom I love!
The sky is summer-blue,
And meadows full of buttercups
Are spread abroad for you.

METHOD

Level – Moderate ❀ ❀

Do you like butter? Little girls will not need to hold buttercups under their chins to decide whether they like the Buttercup Fairy's sumptuous frock—the answer is sure to be an enthusiastic yes. For a look as rich as freshly churned butter, use a yellow fabric with a sheen, such as satin, dupion or polished cotton sateen. Details such as a neckline decked with leaves and a delicate, tasselled hem make this dress fit for a fairy. Green tights, dainty slippers and a posy of buttercups will complete the Buttercup Fairy's look.

SIZE: Measurements and templates
to fit a 4–5 year-old child.

MATERIALS:

❀ 2 m (2 yd) yellow fabric

❀ green stretch jersey fabric

❀ gold metallic thread

❀ narrow waistband elastic

❀ Velcro®

❀ leaves and stamens from
   artificial flowers

❀ green tights and slippers

UNDERSLIP

1. To make the underslip, lay a child's vest wrong-side out on a piece of folded green stretch jersey fabric. Draw around the vest, allowing extra length so that the underslip reaches the middle of the child's thighs and adding an extra 5 cm (2 in) all round for seams. Cut out the pieces, then sew up the shoulders and sides and turn the slip right-side out.

2. Tear the leaves off artificial flowers and pin them around the neckline of the underslip. Sew the leaves in place. Slash up from the bottom of the underslip about 12 cm (5 in) all around to make a fringed hem.

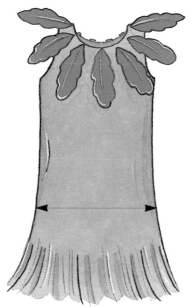

3. Cut two strips of yellow fabric, each measuring 5 cm x 1 m (2 in x 1 yd). Fold down along the length of these two strips so that right sides are facing. Stitch down the length, leaving approximately 1.5 cm ($^1/_2$ in) from the fold line and catching both layers to form a tube.

4. Close off one end of each yellow tube. Turn the tubes right-side out by poking a pencil through the middle. Roll each tube between your fingers to form a rounded shape.

5. Cut each tube into roughly 10 cm (4 in) lengths. Poke a few stamens into the open end of each tube and glue the end closed with a hot glue gun.

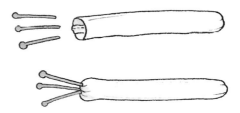

6. Intersperse these yellow stems evenly around the fringe and sew them in place, so they hang just below the hem.

DRESS

1. Using the template provided, make a paper pattern for the skirt petals.

2. Mark five skirt petals on to the yellow fabric and cut them out.

3. Make another pattern for the bodice petals, using the template provided. Mark out five of these smaller, pointed petals on to the yellow fabric and cut them out.

4. Using gold metallic thread, sew around the curved outline of the petals with a decorative zigzag stitch.

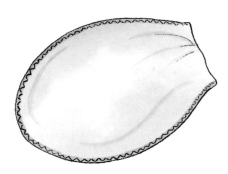

5. Lay out the five large skirt petals, slightly overlapping, and sew a gathering stitch along the straight edge. Do the same for the bodice petals.

6. Lay the bodice petals on top of the skirt petals with right sides together. Sew together at the waist seam, slightly easing the gathers as you go.

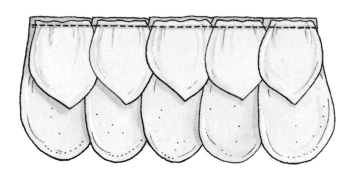

7. Fit narrow elastic to the child's waist, allowing ease of fit but enough tightness to cinch in the waist. Using zigzag stitch, sew the elastic to the seam allowance where the bodice and skirt petals join on the reverse of the fabric.

8. Have the child try on the petal dress and find where the petals overlap. Pin some Velcro® in this position at the waist seam, then sew in place.

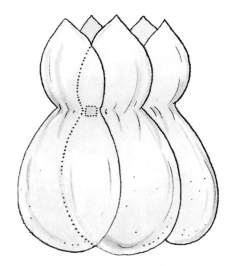

9. Put the green vest inside the petal skirt. Pull the bodice petals up and pin them in place around the neckline. Sew each bodice petal to the vest at one or two points.

WINGS

The Buttercup Fairy's wings were made from clear, yellow acetate, using the method on pages 12–15. Fingerpaint the yellow acetate with large dots of black acrylic paint, abstract streaks of green and black paint and accents of pale blue. Stick thin strips of bright yellow tissue paper to the wings with a very diluted solution of glitter glue and water.

THE CHRISTMAS TREE FAIRY

The little Christmas Tree was born
And dwelt in open air;
It did not guess how bright a dress
Some day its boughs would wear;
Brown cones were all, it thought, a tall
And grown-up Fir would bear.

O little Fir! Your forest home
Is far and far away;
And here indoors these boughs of yours
With coloured balls are gay,
With candle-light, and tinsel bright,
For this is Christmas Day!

A dolly-fairy stands on top,
Till children sleep; then she
(A live one now!) from bough to bough
Goes gliding silently.
O magic sight, this joyous night!
O laden, sparkling tree!

METHOD
Level – Moderate ❀ ❀

At Christmas time, the fir tree sparkles with tinsel, twinkling candles and colourful baubles, but the Christmas Tree Fairy is the loveliest ornament of all. A frilly confection of snowy tulle and shimmering organza, this dress is a Christmas wish come true. Best of all, it uses a white vest for the bodice, reducing the amount of sewing involved. Waving a magic wand and crowned with a glittering tiara, whoever wears this costume will be the star of any yuletide celebration.

SIZE: Measurements and templates to fit a 6–7 year-old child.

MATERIALS:

❀ 1.5 m (1¹/₂ yd) crystal white organza

❀ 2 m (2 yd) white tulle (net)

❀ 4 m (4 yd) green ribbon

❀ clear plastic rod

❀ 1 reel of silver thread

❀ 1 white vest or leotard

❀ child's green headband

❀ 50 cm (20 in) waistband elastic, 2.5 cm (1 in) wide

❀ silver and green glitter, sequins or hologram card

$\mathcal{V}$EST

1. Cut two strips of crystal organza, each measuring 18 cm (7 in) by the width of the fabric, for the sleeve frills.

2. Fold the organza strips in half lengthwise and gently press the crease in with a cool iron.

3. Using the creases as guidelines, sew a gathering stitch along the length of each crease, so that the frills fit the vest's armholes.

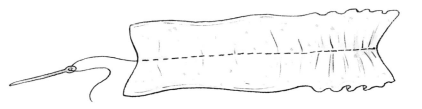

4. Trim the ends of the frills so they taper around the armholes.

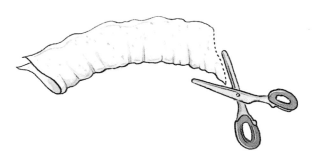

5. Open out a frill and pin it on to the right side of one armhole. Arrange the gathers evenly along the armhole and pin the frill in place. Attach the second frill to the other armhole in the same way.

6. Place the vest and frill on the sewing machine and set it to a small stitch size (i.e. 2). Starting at the underarm, stretch out the vest slightly and stitch around

the armhole elastic along the frill's centre crease. Do the same for the second frill and armhole.

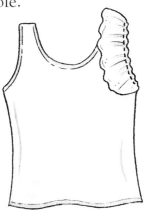

7. Finish off the frill edges by sewing along them with a small zigzag stitch using silver metallic thread. For an easier option, trim the edges with pinking shears or paint along the edges with silver glitter paint to seal any fraying.

8. Make the neck frill in the same way, but cut a frill 2.5 cm (1 in) wide by twice the vest's neckline measurement.

9. Attach a length of green ribbon to each shoulder of the vest, criss-cross the ribbons over the chest and back, and tie the ends together at the waist.

SKIRT

1. Measure the child's skirt length from the waist to just above the knee. Cut two pieces of crystal organza to this measurement along the width of the fabric.

2. For the underskirt, cut two pieces of white tulle, adding 2 cm (1 in) to the length of the organza pieces but using the same width.

3. Cut a piece of waistband elastic to fit the child's waist measurement minus 10 cm (4 in), then check it for fit.

4. Cut a strip of crystal organza long enough to cover the elastic waistband, adding an extra 4 cm (1½ in) to the width for seam allowance.

5. Press a fold line lengthwise along the centre of the organza strip. Stitch along the long, non-folded edge, catching both layers, to make a channel. Attach a safety pin to one end of the elastic and thread it through the channel, ruching up the fabric as you go. Pin the ends of the elastic to the ends of the channel, then sew them together. Sew the ends of the organza channel to finish the waistband.

6. Place the two organza skirt pieces on top of each other with right sides facing and sew each of the short ends together to form a tube. Turn the tube right-side out. Repeat this step for the tulle underskirt.

7. Place the underskirt inside the organza overskirt. Using the longest machine stitch, run a gathering stitch close to the top edge of the skirt, catching both the over and under skirts. Pull the ends of the thread to form gathers.

8. Pull out the elastic waistband to its fullest and pin on the gathered edge of the skirt. As you pin, arrange the gathers to fall evenly around the skirt. Sew around the waistband, stretching the elastic out as you work.

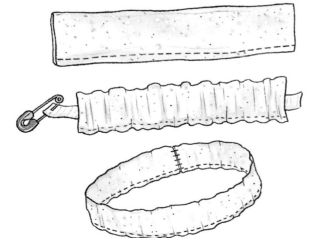

9. Finish the skirt hems with zigzag stitch using metallic silver thread. Alternately, paint the hems with silver metallic paint or trim them with pinking shears.

10. Stitch a length of green ribbon approximately 60 cm (2 ft) longer than the child's waist around the waistband, leaving the ends loose at the back of the skirt. Tie the loose ends of the ribbon in a bow.

Headband

1. Using the template provided, trace a star shape on to a piece of thick card and cut it out.

2. Cover the star with silver glitter, sequins or hologram card, then stick it to the centre of a child's green headband with a glue gun.

Wand

1. As for the headband, draw two star shapes on to a piece of thick card and cut them out. Cover both stars' front sides with glitter, sequins or hologram card.

2. Glue green glitter on to a clear plastic rod. Alternately, you could cover a dowelling with green ribbon.

3. Sandwich the tip of the rod between the two stars and secure using a glue gun.

Wings

The Christmas Tree Fairy's spectacular multi-coloured wings were created with a combination of paints and tissue paper. Follow the instructions on pages 12–15 to make and decorate the wings. Colourful wings adorned with strips of yellow tissue paper and pastel pink, green and blue paint streaks enliven the Christmas Tree Fairy's white outfit. For added colour, you could also tie a piece of green ribbon around the centre of the wings and let the ends trail down the child's back.

THE POPPY FAIRY

The green wheat's a-growing,
The lark sings on high;
In scarlet silk a-glowing,
Here stand I.

The wheat's turning yellow,
Ripening for sheaves;
I hear the little fellow
Who scares the bird-thieves.

Now the harvest's ended,
The wheat-field is bare;
But still, red and splendid,
I am there.

METHOD
Level – Moderate ❀ ❀

In her stunning scarlet gown, the Poppy Fairy stands out like a flame in golden wheat fields. This ethereal dress combines crimson organza with accents of black net and glittering sequins. A pompom headband crowns this striking ensemble. Wearing this floaty dress, girls will be equally prepared to flutter barefoot through a meadow or enchant guests at a summer party.

SIZE: Measurements and templates to fit a 7–8 year-old child.

MATERIALS:

❀ 3 m (3 yd) red organza

❀ ¹/₂ m (¹/₂ yd) black flocked net

❀ green spotted net

❀ 1 m (1 yd) red stretch lining (or red swimsuit/leotard)

❀ 1 m (1 yd) waistband elastic

❀ roll of nylon fishing line

❀ black sequins

❀ black marker pen

❀ black fabric paint

❀ child's green headband

❀ black artificial flower stamens

❀ fabric glue

DRESS

1. Fold the red organza in half lengthwise, then fold it three times in a concertina, to create six layers. The length of this folded piece should equal the length of the child from waist to mid-calf.

2. Mark out a semicircular shape from corner to corner on the folded fabric, then cut around the shape, including the straight edge. This should make six semicircular petals.

3. Make a waistband (as shown on page 10) and cover the elastic with red stretch lining fabric.

4. Gather each petal along its straight edge until it measures just over one quarter of the child's waist measurement.

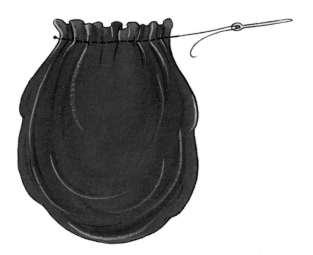

5. Fold the elastic waistband in half and press it flat. Mark the four folds with pins to make equally spaced balance points.

6. Take four of the petals and fold the gathered edges in half. Attach the petals at these folds to the four balance points on the elastic. Pin the petals all around the waistband, stretching out the elastic as you work.

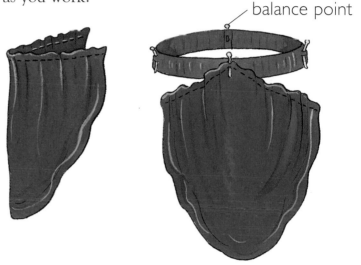

balance point

7. Pulling out the elastic as you go, sew the four petals to the waistband. The front and back petals should slightly overlap the two side petals and lie on top of them.

8. To form the bodice, sew the gathered edges of the two remaining petals to the front and back of the waistband. The curved hem of the petals should point up, rather than down.

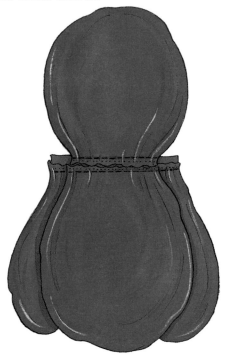

9. Neaten off the waistband seams with zigzag stitch.

10. To make a fluted hem, roll the edge of an organza petal into a small hem, sandwiching a length of fishing line inside the hem. Sew the hem with zigzag stitch, catching the fishing line inside the stitches and slightly stretching the fabric as you work. Do this for each petal.

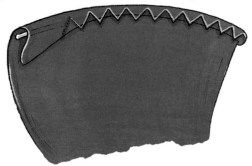

11. Using a marker pen, draw lines on the petals radiating from the centre front of the waistband. Do the same with shiny black fabric paint. Stick black sequins on the front petals with fabric glue, to resemble a scattering of poppy seeds.

12. To make the underslip, lay a child's vest wrong-side out on a piece of folded red stretch lining fabric. Cut out around the vest, allowing an extra 5 cm (2 in) all round for seams. For an easier option, use a red swimsuit or leotard instead of making the underslip.

13. Sew up the shoulders and sides of the underslip, leaving the armholes open, then turn it right-side out.

Belt

14. Fit the underslip on the child and put the petal skirt on top. Pull up the front and back bodice petals and pin them in place on the shoulders of the underslip.

15. Remove the dress and sew the bodice petals to the shoulders of the underslip at the points where pinned.

16. Sew the front and back bodice petals together at the sides with a few hand stitches.

1. Fold a piece of black flocked net, measuring approximately 30 cm x 1 m (12 in x 1 yd), lengthwise into a concertina fan. Catch the concertina in the middle with a pin or paper clip.

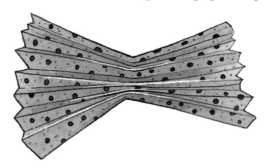

2. Cut another piece of black net, measuring approximately 20 cm x 1 m (8 in x 1 yd), to make a belt. Tie the belt tightly around the concertina's middle, removing the pin or paper clip.

3. Cut along the folds of the concertina fan to make ribbons.

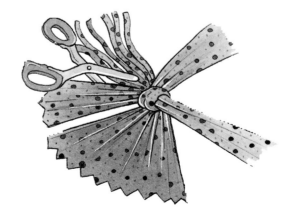

4. Gently pull the ribbons to fill out the pompom shape, and trim them to the desired length.

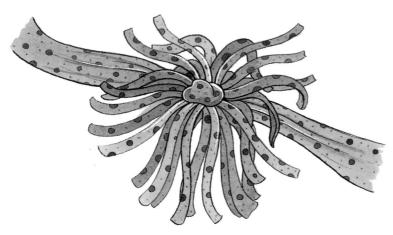

5. Stick black sequins on to the ribbons at the pompom's centre. Tie the belt around the waist of the dress.

Headband

1. Cut ten 15 cm (6 in) squares of green net. Do the same with black net.

2. Take five squares of each colour and lay them on top of each other, alternating green and black.

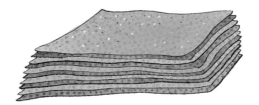

3. As for the belt, fold the layered net concertina style until it forms a fan shape. Pin the fan in the centre, then tie it off tightly with some strong thread.

4. Open out the folded sections and snip into the folds to make ribbon-like strips.

5. Gently pull the strips open to make a puffball shape and trim them to the desired length. Repeat steps 2–5 to make a second puffball.

6. Attach the puffballs to either side of a child's green headband using a hot glue gun.

7. For an extra finishing touch, stick black artificial flower stamens to the centre of each puffball with a glue gun.

Wings

The Poppy Fairy's wings were made from clear acetate using the method explained on pages 12–15. Featuring the same stunning black and red combination used in the Poppy Fairy's dress, these wings are great fun to fingerpaint. Begin by painting rough, black stripes horizontally across the wings. When the black paint has dried, thickly outline the edges of the wings with red paint. For more elaborate wings, glue on black sequins or thin strips of black net.

THE HOLLY FAIRY

O, I am green in Winter-time,
When other trees are brown;
Of all the trees (So saith the rhyme)
The holly bears the crown.
December days are drawing near
When I shall come to town,
And carol-boys go singing clear
Of all the trees (O hush and hear!)
The holly bears the crown!

For who so well-beloved and merry
As the scarlet Holly Berry?

METHOD
Level – Moderate ❀ ❀

Like an elfin court jester, the jolly Holly Fairy brightens up the winter gloom with evergreen leaves and crimson berries. Ideal attire for Christmas parties or New Year celebrations, this costume uses PVC fabric to imitate the texture of holly's prickly leaves and shiny berries. From the cowl to the anklets, this ensemble is picture perfect from head to toe. A touch of blusher for rosy, wind-blown cheeks and a bough of holly will transform the wearer into the merry Holly Fairy.

SIZE: Measurements and templates to fit a 5–6 year-old child.

MATERIALS:

❀ Velcro®

❀ black marker pen

❀ cotton balls

❀ 1 m x 120 cm (1 yd x 4 ft) green stretch velour or stretch satin

❀ 75 cm (30 in) green PVC

❀ 50 cm (20 in) red PVC

❀ 50 cm (20 in) green felt

❀ narrow, green ribbon

❀ wide, black waistband elastic

❀ fabric glue

❀ flower-making wire

❀ red tights or leggings

SKIRT

1. Using the template provided, cut out six holly leaves from green felt. Place the leaves on newspaper and spread with fabric glue on one side. Stick the leaves on to the wrong side of shiny green PVC. When the glue has dried, cut the leaves out of the PVC.

2. Using your finger, press a fold down the middle of each leaf and sew a narrow ridge along each fold.

3. Open out the leaves and stick a length of flower-making wire along the ridge on the PVC side of each leaf. Glue a length of green ribbon on top of each wire.

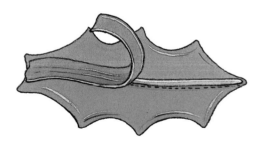

4. Measure the child's waist and cut a waistband 10 cm (4 in) deep from green PVC, adding 20 cm (8 in) extra to the waist measurement for the wrapover.

5. Fold the waistband in half lengthwise and sew along the long, unfolded edge. Attach a piece of Velcro,® approximately 7 cm (2 3/4 in) long, to each end, making sure the Velcro® pieces match up.

6. Fix the leaves along the waistband, slightly overlapping each other. Sew each leaf down either side of its spine about 5 cm (2 in) to attach it to the waistband.

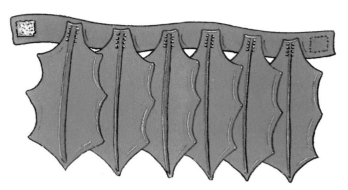

7. Using the large circle template, cut out seven circles from red fabric. Hand sew a loose running stitch around each circle. Stuff the centre of each circle with cotton balls. Pull the thread to form a ball and fasten off tightly.

8. Attach the berries to the waistband between each holly leaf using fabric glue or hand stitch. With a black marker pen, draw a small cross on the top of each berry.

THE FUCHSIA FAIRY

Fuchsia is a dancer
Dancing on her toes,
Clad in red and purple,
By a cottage wall;
Sometimes in a greenhouse,
In frilly white and rose,
Dressed in her best for the fairies' evening ball!

METHOD
Level – Advanced ❀ ❀ ❀

This gorgeous Fuchsia Fairy costume will dance its way into every young ballerina's affections. Luxurious shot silk dupion provides rich colour and the stiffness required for this costume, but it is possible to use less expensive material, such as synthetic silk, taffeta lining or even furnishing fabric. When little girls don this dress, they will be ready to twirl the night away at the fairy ball!

SIZE: Measurements and templates to fit a 5–6 year-old child.

MATERIALS:

❀ 2 m (1 yd) pink shot silk dupion

❀ 1.25 m (1¼ yd) purple shot silk dupion

❀ scraps of stiff net

❀ Velcro®

❀ pink artificial flower stamens

❀ fabric glue

❀ 50 cm (20 in) waistband elastic, 2 cm (1 in) wide

❀ 50 cm (20 in) waistband elastic, 4 cm (2 in) wide

STEMS AND BUDS

1. Using the pink fabric, follow steps 3–4 for the Buttercup Fairy on page 31. Cut the fabric tubes into ten stems.

2. For the buds, cut out ten circles of pink fabric with 12 cm (5 in) diameters. Cut each circle in half to make 20 semicircles.

3. Place two semicircles on a table with their straight edges facing you. Fold each corner into the middle of the curved edge to form a point.

4. Pinch the two folded pieces in place and hold them together with their folds facing outwards. Push the end of a pink stem between the two pinched pieces.

5. Sandwiching the stem and the two folded semicircle pieces together, sew a loose gathering stitch, catching all layers of the semicircles and the stem. Pull the ends of the thread tightly to cinch in the tops of the semicircles.

6. With a hot glue gun or fabric glue, place a blob of glue on the stitching. Stick some artificial stamens on to the end of the stem if you have them.

7. Pull up the two semicircular pieces, bringing the points together. Pinch the two sides around the glued, stitched end of the stem to form an enclosed bud.

8. Repeat steps 3–7 to make all ten buds.

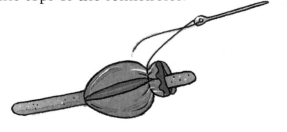

TEMPLATES

ENLARGING TEMPLATES

The templates featured on the following pages are drawn to a half of their actual size. To enlarge them to full size, you will need to use dressmakers' grid paper ruled with 1 cm (³/8 in) squares. One square on the grid in this book equals four squares on the dressmakers' grid paper. Mark out the template on the dressmakers' grid paper, using the boxes as guidelines. Use a ruler to connect straight edges and draw curved lines freehand. Cut out your paper pattern.

I square on the template = 4 squares on dressmakers' grid paper

ALTERING TEMPLATES

The templates included in this book are intended to fit the age of child specified in the introduction to each costume. Most of the templates are one-size-fits-all, but a few you will need to alter if you wish to make the costume for an older or younger child. An easy way to do this is using a photocopier with an enlarging facility. Simply make a copy of the full-size template to the correct percentage larger or smaller. Alternately, templates can be adjusted manually. First, enlarge the template to full size, as described above. To alter a template's width or length, cut along the dotted adjustment lines on the template. Stick a piece of paper between the two halves to the required size, then draw in lines to connect the template pieces. Cut out the altered pattern. To reduce a template's width or length, pin a fold to the required amount along the dotted adjustment lines, then cut out the pattern.

CUTTING OUT PATTERNS

Pin the patterns to the fabric to hold them in place. To use the fabric economically, interlock the pieces where possible and leave approximately 10 cm (4 in) between each piece. When cutting out stretch fabrics, always ensure that the stretch runs widthways across the piece. Cut the pieces out with sharp scissors. If you need to cut around the same pattern more than once, trace around it with tailor's chalk. Reposition the pattern and repin it to the fabric.

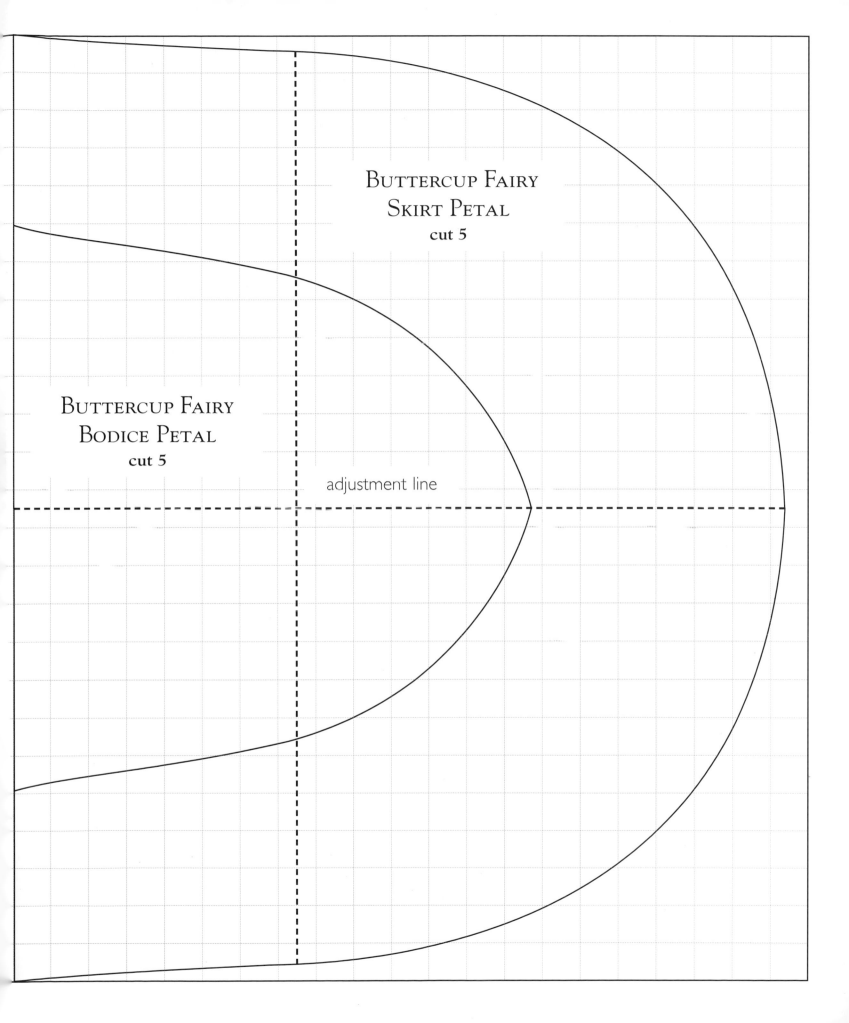

BUTTERCUP FAIRY
SKIRT PETAL
cut 5

BUTTERCUP FAIRY
BODICE PETAL
cut 5

adjustment line

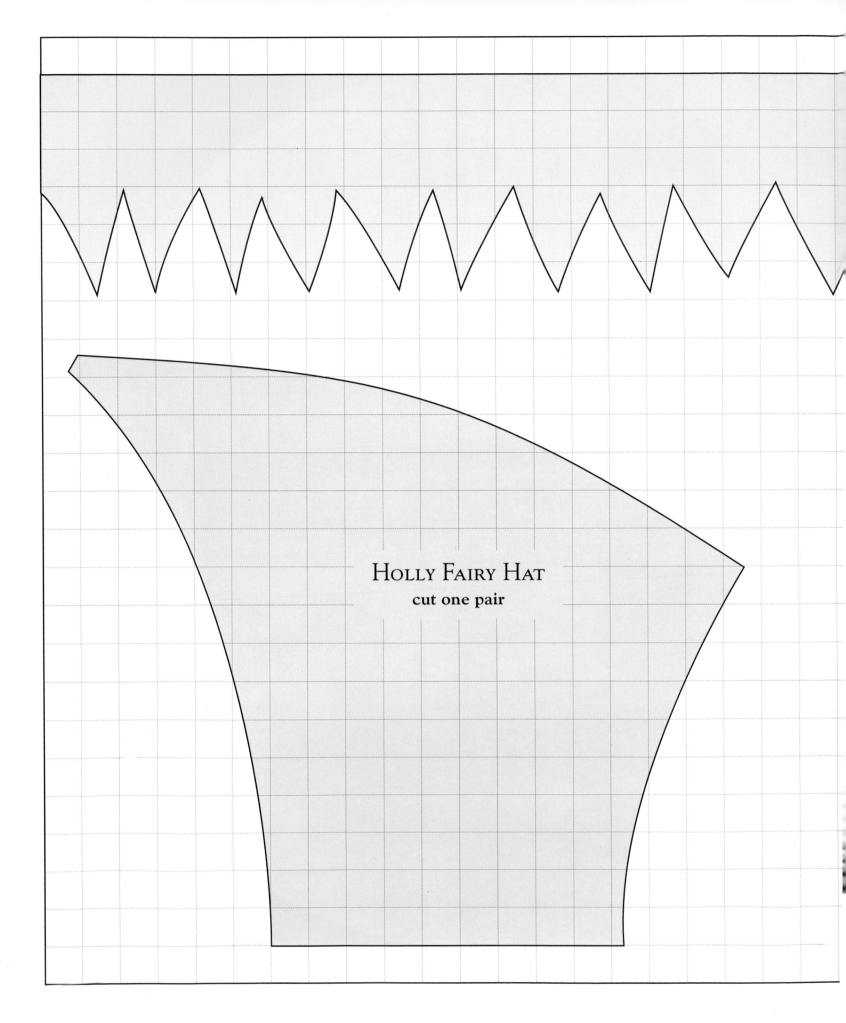

HOLLY FAIRY HAT
cut one pair

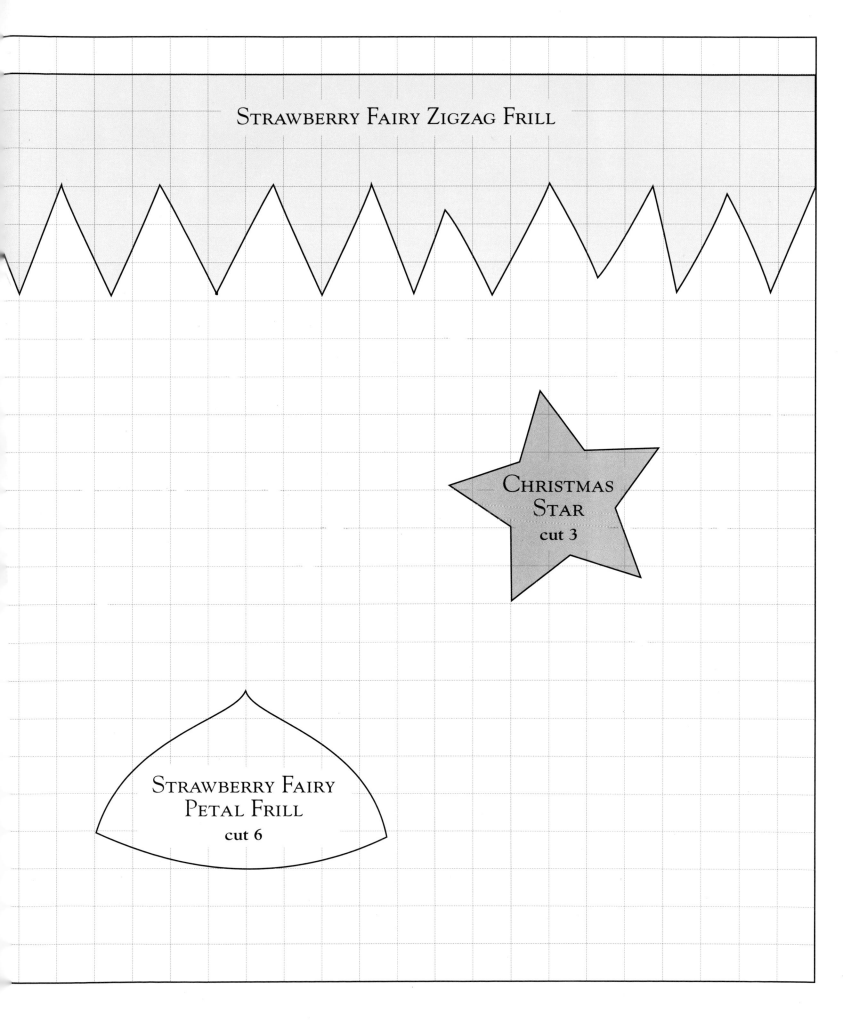

Strawberry Fairy Zigzag Frill

Christmas
Star
cut 3

Strawberry Fairy
Petal Frill
cut 6

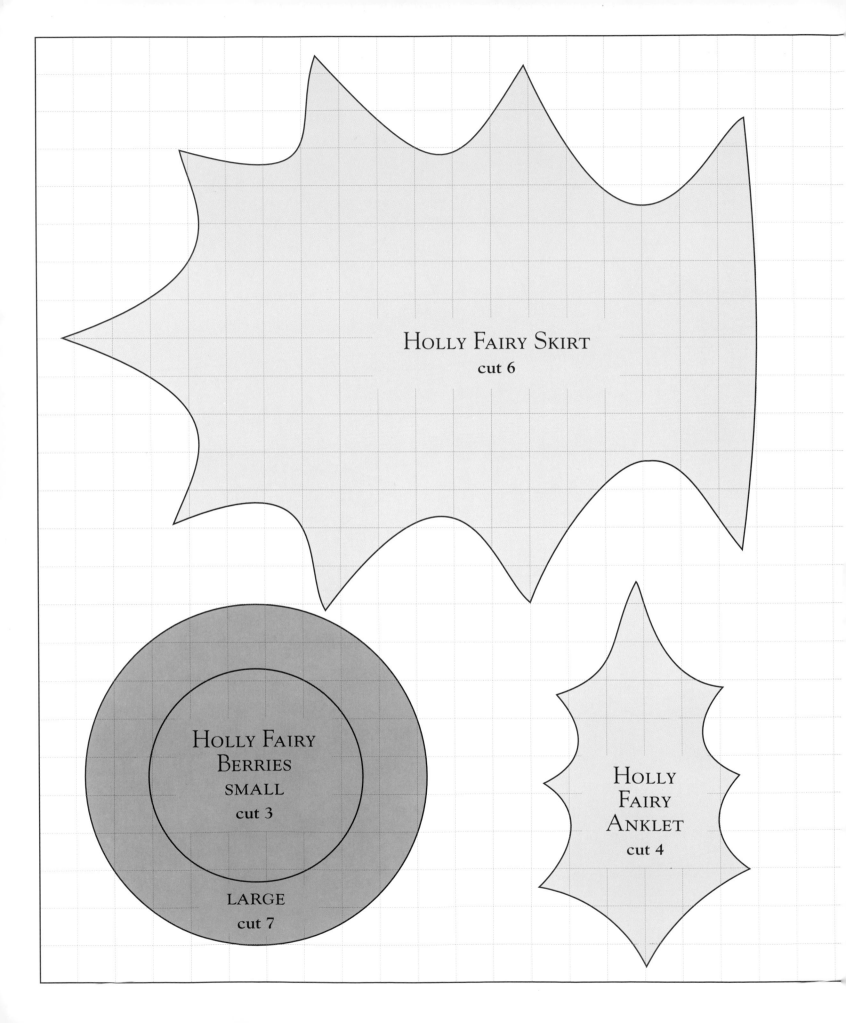

Holly Fairy Skirt

cut 6

Holly Fairy
Berries

SMALL

cut 3

LARGE

cut 7

Holly
Fairy
Anklet

cut 4

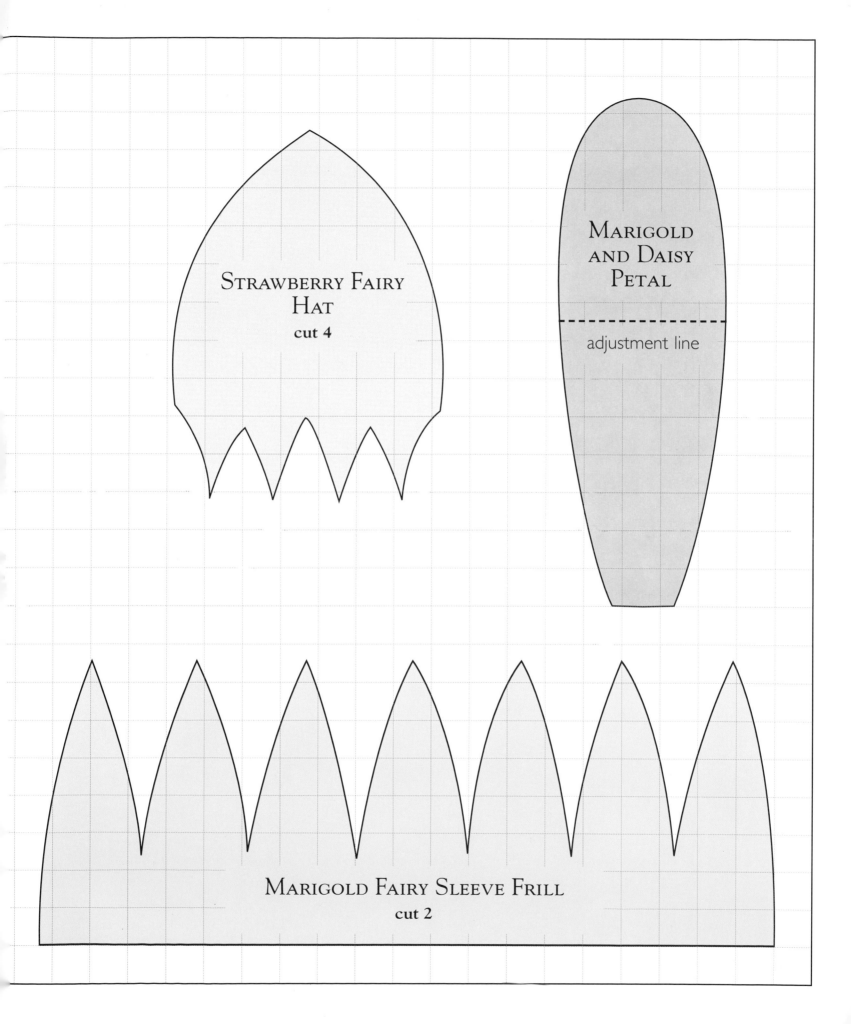

Strawberry Fairy Hat

cut 4

Marigold and Daisy Petal

adjustment line

Marigold Fairy Sleeve Frill

cut 2